N

DATE DUE

FEB 1 3 1985		
4/10/06		

HIGHSMITH 45-220

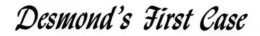

Desmond's First Case

Also by Herbert Best

Desmond's First Case

by HERBERT BEST

Illustrated by EZRA JACK KEATS

THE VIKING PRESS · NEW YORK

To Martha D.,

alumna of Orphans of the Storm, *who has made humans her life study, and whose research has enabled me to write this story.*

Desmond's First Case

Chapter 1

This was Desmond's first case. When it all began he had no idea that it would launch him on an exciting career.

Of course, Desmond hadn't given much thought to his future career. Just being dog to Gus was a full-time job in itself because Gus picked up adventure the way Desmond picked up mud and burrs. Gus was a smart little guy.

They were sitting on the front steps, Desmond and his boy Gus, wishing that every day in the year could look so promising, and wondering what kind of adventure would fit so lovely a morning.

"It'll have to be something extra special," said Gus, thinking what Desmond was thinking.

That was true; it would have to be. Last week they had wandered into a field looking for black-caps for Gus's mother, and the next thing they knew they were flying over a five-bar gate with a bull snorting behind them. Something like that would do nicely.

Desmond laid his shiny black head on Gus's knee and waved his bushy black tail with the white end, to catch his attention. Bill the boxer lived only two houses down the street. Gus could go along and catch Bill's attention while Desmond slipped in quietly and grabbed Bill's bone. Bill always had a bone. Then Bill could chase Desmond and the bone while Gus got safely away. If they played the same game on two or three dogs at two or three houses it would get things moving nicely.

But for once Gus couldn't understand what Desmond was thinking. He didn't seem interested in bones.

Well then, here was another idea. Desmond was full of them this morning. How about going round to Mr. Titus next door?

"I know what! We'll go see Mr. Titus." Gus jumped up. "He's always thinking of new things. He calls it inventing. He'll invent an adventure for us, easy as easy. You see if he doesn't."

Desmond trotted after Gus. It wasn't a bad idea at all. Even the first time they had met Mr. Titus had been a sort of adventure. That was all of two years ago. They'd been hunting rhino, which was make-believe and kid's stuff, and they didn't do it any more. The rhino made a snorting noise, the way a rhino does before he charges through a lilac hedge, and Gus stopped him in his tracks with an arrow from his bow. Only the rhino was a lawnmower and the arrow just missed the man behind it. The rhino stopped snorting because Mr. Titus switched off the engine.

Desmond went through the hedge to say it was their arrow. The best thing to do when you are in trouble is to get it over with.

But there wasn't any trouble. The arrow had broken on the mower and Mr. Titus mended it for them. What's more, he fixed rubber cups to all the arrows, so that if you shot them at the big garage door they stuck there.

Now Gus and Desmond slipped through the gap in the lilac hedge, trotted across the lawn, which needed mowing, and headed for the garage. Just lately, since he'd retired—which it seemed was like taking an endless vacation—Mr. Titus didn't go to work at the bank any longer, and was almost always in his garage inventing things. His car stood outside the garage as usual because there was no room for it inside.

Gus went round to the little side door and tried the padlock. Then they both looked in through the window. There were lots of machines inside, but no Mr. Titus.

"He must have gone for a walk," said Gus. "Let's us go down to the drugstore."

So they went. It's a good plan to fill up your stomach before starting an adventure. It's like gassing up your car.

On their way they passed Gloria the German sheep-dog, herding no less than five small children and keeping them safe on the sidewalk. No other dog in town could handle more than two or three, but sheep-herding was Gloria's family's profession. It came to her naturally.

Then there was Sally the spaniel, her nose and long ears sweeping the ground as she followed the scent of a mole from one yard to the next. She never cared what she followed as long as she followed something. Sally had a single-track mind.

Desmond envied them, in a way. It was fine to know just where your talents lay and to follow them. But when a dog had as many mixed ancestors as Desmond had, he naturally had a lot of talents. So it was hard to know where to use them all. It was like Gus's having to decide if he'd be a great scientist and land on Venus or be a pitcher for the Yankees.

They turned in at the drugstore with its shiny long counter and mixture of strange smells. Dogs weren't usually allowed inside, but Desmond was special, ever since he had pointed out the kitten in the chestnut tree outside and Gus had shinned up and rescued her. She was the drugstore kitten and now she was the drugstore cat. She came out from behind the counter to speak to Desmond.

Gus ordered a triple-dip ice-cream cone, and Desmond sat down beside his stool, to remind him that he expected the end of the cone with a little ice cream still in it. Gus was a generous little guy.

People in the drugstore were talking. People talk the way a dog chews a bone—just to keep the jaw muscles limber—and Desmond always listened in case they came to a bit of marrow.

A man with a chocolate malted said, "Sure he's a banker—that is, he was until he retired a couple of weeks ago. But he didn't light out with any of the bank's money. That's what they don't understand."

A plump lady with a big banana split said, "Likely he's just visiting relatives. I don't tell the cops every time I go see my daughter at Bayview. It's a free country."

A thin girl with a cup of black coffee said, "He's lost his memory; happens all the time."

And Mr. James behind the counter had his own idea. "Gangsters. Sure as sure. Kidnaped, he was. There'll be a ransom note soon," he said, and punched the cash register.

Gus was listening so hard he almost finished the last bit of his ice-cream cone. But Desmond nudged his elbow to remind him not to—and to remind him too that they shouldn't waste the whole day in listening to human talk when there was adventure waiting for them somewhere else. So they went out again.

Ahead of them a friend of Gus's was delivering the afternoon papers from a bicycle. He was out of practice, and one of his papers missed the doorway and landed on the sidewalk. Gus picked it up, because it might get dirty. Then he looked at the headlines.

He let out a whistle of surprise. Desmond pricked up his ears.

"What those guys were talking about," said Gus, "must be true. It's all here in the *Newtown Gazette*. Missing Banker!"

Desmond said nothing, but his nose tingled, just as it did when he picked up an interesting scent.

"Know what we're going to do, you old dog, you?" Gus slung the paper neatly into the doorway. Then he did a kind of dance right there on the sidewalk. "We're going to follow the trail of this missing banker and find him!"

There would be just time for that before lunch—or should have been. But when they got to Mr. Titus's house it looked as though he had visitors and wouldn't be able to talk about finding trails. There were three other cars in his drive; one of them had a sticker on it that said "Press," and another was the kind the state troopers use.

Desmond and Gus were ducking through the lilac hedge on their way back home when Gus said suddenly, "Mr. Titus is a banker, isn't he? What'll you bet he's missing and that's why the troopers are there?"

Desmond's nose tingled so much that he had to sneeze. Mr. Titus was their next-door neighbor and friend, and

Desmond and Gus ought to have looked after him better, and not let him get lost. What they had to do now was to find him and bring him back.

Here they were, with their noses right on the start of the trail. The trail of *the missing banker!*

Chapter 2

Desmond and Gus had eaten dinner and were sitting on the front-porch steps. They felt a little troubled, which isn't the way you ought to feel if your dinner agrees with you. They were trying to think where Mr. Titus could have gone, so they could go after him and find him. But though Gus asked Desmond, and Desmond looked inquiringly at Gus, neither of them seemed to know.

A tall state trooper in shiny black leggings and smart blue uniform came around the end of the house. He must have discovered that gap in the hedge.

Desmond always liked troopers. Their leather leggings had such an interesting smell, and they weren't afraid when you went up and sniffed at them.

"Your father in, sonny?" the man asked Gus.

Gus showed him into the house and called his father, and came out again to sit down—and to listen, of course.

"I'm from the state police, sir," said the man. "As you are next-door neighbor to Mr. Titus, perhaps you can tell me something about him. And the names and addresses of some of his relatives."

Gus's father said he didn't know of any relatives; in fact, he didn't know Mr. Titus himself very well. Mr. Titus didn't join clubs, or play bridge or golf, and when he'd come back from the bank every afternoon he usually spent most of his time in his workshop.

"So he had no close friends. But how about enemies?"

"I should hardly think he would have any," said Father. "Apart from his banking and his hobbies he seemed to have few interests. But he was a good neighbor."

Desmond gave a shiver. He didn't like the sound of "was."

The trooper wanted details. So Gus's father told about a time that Desmond remembered, too. The television set had gone out of order at the same time that Mr. Titus was using some machinery in his workshop. Desmond and Gus were sent across with a note asking if Mr. Titus would be so kind as not to run his machinery when the World Series was being shown. Mr. Titus had come right over and fixed the TV. Its trouble hadn't been the fault of his machinery, but he said they should not hesitate to call him if it went wrong again. That was really neighborly.

"Well, sir, if you can think of anything that would

help us locate Mr. Titus, please ring us at once. All we have discovered is that his housekeeper says he hasn't slept in his bed or used his car since a week ago last Monday. We know no reason for his disappearance, and there must be at least a thousand people who knew him at the bank, and would recognize him anywhere. Yet nobody has set eyes on him. People don't just vanish into air."

Desmond looked hopefully at Gus, but Gus shook his head in doubt. Yet if the state police couldn't do anything to find Mr. Titus, that was all the more reason why Desmond and Gus should.

This was why, an hour after Gus had gone to bed and all the house was dark, Desmond smelled Gus tiptoeing silently down the stairs. He got up from his mat just as silently and licked Gus's hand to say he was ready and waiting.

Gus had to use his flashlight to unfasten the front door. Then off they went across the dew-wet lawn and through the lilac hedge, remembering all the nice things that Mr. Titus had done for them, from mending this very same flashlight to telling them they could come into the workshop whenever they wanted, so long as they kept quiet and used the hand tools and not the machinery.

His car was still outside the garage, but the other cars had gone. The little side door to the garage was fastened by a padlock, but Mr. Titus had shown them how to open it without a key, because he was always mislaying his own key. You tipped it on its side and jiggled it in a special way.

Gus turned on his flashlight and they went in and looked around. There was no sign of Mr. Titus, though he often worked until quite late at night. Gus went straight to the big lathe where Mr. Titus had been standing when they saw him last. Desmond hoped he wouldn't go too close, as machinery was treacherous stuff. Sometimes it purred, and sometimes it growled, but that didn't mean it was either pleased or angry. Then all of a sudden it grabbed you or bit. But perhaps Gus was safe now, because the machinery seemed to be asleep.

"Know what I've discovered?" Gus whispered. "He finished that job he was on and brushed out the turnings and cleaned up. What have you found, you old dog, you?"

Desmond had sniffed all over the floor and right into

the corners. There were some new smells and one, though it was too faint for him to be certain, might have been the leather polish on the trooper's leggings. Perhaps Mr. Titus's old overalls would tell more. Desmond nosed back the door so he could get a good sniff. And there on the hook where the overalls always hung was—nothing!

Here was a discovery which he really must tell Gus about. There was only one way to do it. Desmond raised one front paw, stuck his tail straight out behind, and pointed with his nose in just the way his great grandmother would have done; she was a famous pointer.

Gus understood at once, because he really was a smart little guy for his weight and age. "Sure, they should be there, because Mr. Titus wouldn't let his housekeeper come in for fear of her tidying up and putting things back in their wrong places. And he always forgot to send them to the laundry. Good old Desmond!"

Now Desmond's discovery put Gus on to another discovery. Since Mr. Titus had too many tools to put away in drawers, a lot of them hung up on the walls. So that he could tell where to put each one back where he could find it again, he had painted its outline on the wall behind it, like a black shadow.

It was Gus's turn to point. Some of the tools were missing, and only their black-painted shadows showed where they should be!

"Somebody's taken them," said Gus, "And the overalls!"

Then they heard footsteps outside in the darkness. Somebody opened the door of Mr. Titus's car. Gus turned off his flashlight, and he and Desmond sneaked to the side door. They had just closed and fastened it behind them when they heard someone rattling the big garage doors as though trying to open them. So it couldn't be Mr. Titus. They were only a few yards away when they heard the man go round and try to open the side door. Then the moon came out a little from behind the clouds, when they most needed darkness. The man must have turned and seen them, for he yelled, "Stop!"

Some people would have raced straight for home; but not Gus. When one of you is supposed to be asleep in bed, and the other guarding the downstairs, you don't lead a policeman—if it was a policeman—home to rouse your father and ask a lot of awkward questions.

You run in the opposite direction. At least Gus did, and Desmond followed. Then Desmond took the lead, because he could run faster and wanted to show a good hiding place in a house that was being torn down. Then he had a better idea. Bulldogs—and he was part bulldog —never ran away. They held a man. Why shouldn't Desmond hold the pursuer by a trouser leg till Gus could get away from him and go home?

Desmond gave a deep growl and turned.

"No, Desmond, no!" Gus forgot to whisper. He almost yelled. "He may shoot you!"

Desmond had never been shot yet, so he wasn't afraid of shooting. But he remembered that from nearby the man would see his beautiful white "shirt front." A black dog with a shining white front would be easy to describe, and there was only one on this side of town—Desmond himself! Anyone could tell the policeman—if it *was* a policeman—where Desmond lived, and that he and Gus were always together. And then it would come out that Gus had slipped out of bed, and there would be serious trouble.

It was really worrying. It was so late that the streets were deserted and there was no hope of a crowd to dodge into and lose yourself among. And every friendly door was shut and locked. Gus could certainly run, but his legs weren't very much longer than Desmond's, and he had only two of them. And of course the policeman

or gangster, or whoever the Sinister Stranger was, had started to catch up.

Something must be done.

Desmond slowed down, so the Sinister Stranger slowed down too. That gave Gus time to get farther ahead. But almost at once the Sinister Stranger must have noticed that only Desmond was in sight. So he put on speed again.

Now for the trick! Just at the corner of the Congregational Church, Desmond made a sharp turn. He even remembered to give the white tip of his tail a wave so that the stranger would notice. Lots of dogs had white tips on their tails, so that didn't matter. What did matter was that the man thought Desmond was still following Gus, so he followed Desmond round the corner—just as Desmond had planned!

Now it was going to be easy. The Sinister Stranger wore a raincoat and a hat, but even if he had been stripped for running Desmond could have led him all round Robin Hood's barn and back again, while Gus sauntered comfortably home to bed.

At a slow trot, so the man wouldn't get discouraged and give up the chase, Desmond led him through the outskirts of town. He grinned to himself as he wondered whether to lead the Sinister Stranger through a wet plowed field or through the deeper mud beside a milking shed. He had just decided on the milking shed, because it would give the man a nice strong scent which would make it easy to recognize him afterward, when he heard a whistle behind him.

It came again—Gus's private whistle, *Whee-a-whee.* The stranger heard it too, and stopped dead.

Desmond barked, "Look out!" Gus ought to have known the meaning of the warning after all these years. Yet out of the darkness came the whistle, again and again, just as often as Gus could find breath. And it was drawing nearer all the time.

Gus didn't intend to run home and leave his dog in danger!

Now the man must have seen Gus, for he turned and ran. Gus must have seen the man, for he stopped whistling and ran too. Now it was Sinister Stranger chasing Gus, and Desmond chasing Sinister Stranger. Desmond couldn't pass the stranger, or he might be recognized, but he put on speed and drew closer, ready to spring and hold the man by his raincoat if Gus was in danger.

But Gus could use his head as well as his legs. The hunt, which had dropped to half run and half walk by now, reached the Congregational Church but instead of turning down Main Street crossed right over. Yes, Gus must have had the same idea that Desmond had way back.

The Sinister Stranger went right on past a tumble-down house across the street from the church. Desmond followed so that he would not arouse his suspicion.

Then, safely past, he dropped back, picked up Gus's scent, and followed it down a plank into the old cellar hole. In the darkness he gave Gus a lick to say how smart the little fellow was, and waited.

The man came puffing back, very out of breath, and they both got a good view of him—just an ordinary-looking man in a raincoat with a soft hat pulled down over his ears. He certainly wasn't a trooper, but he might be a detective—or a gangster!

The people in the drugstore had talked about kid-naping, and this might be a member of the gang who had been sent with a demand note for Mr. Titus's ransom and was trying to find someone to give it to.

The hair on Desmond's back stood up till Gus laid a hand on him to soothe him. Gus didn't understand that the first thing a pup is taught by his mother is Never Trust a Stranger.

They waited in the darkness while the stranger walked round the wrecked house twice. He started round again and fell over something. He picked himself up and went off grumbling.

After they got home and Gus had crept upstairs to bed, it was a long time before Desmond could settle down. He kept pattering around and listening at doors and windows. With Sinister Strangers around at night you couldn't be too careful of bolts and locks. Desmond even checked on the refrigerator door while he was about it.

Chapter 3

"Mr. Titus is a friend of ours," Gus pointed out next morning. "So we've got to find him, dead or alive."

Desmond said nothing, because he was doing a lot of thinking.

This was a fine place to think in, here under the porch where the bean poles, flowerpots, and such things were stored away. It wasn't perhaps as good a place as the old woodshed, but everybody knew that was where Gus did most of his thinking, and it didn't do to take chances with the Sinister Stranger hovering around. Also, there seemed to be quite a lot of kids who had nothing better to do than go around yelling "Gus! Anybody seen Gus? Hi, Gus! What you doing now, Gus? Wanna play ball, Gus?"

Gus squatted on one of the bigger flowerpots, took off his cap, scratched his head, and began to think—out loud, of course, so Desmond could hear him and maybe help.

"Trouble is how to set about finding Mr. Titus. And that's where you come in, you old dog, you. You've found lost baseballs, you've found dropped pencils. You've even found things as small as a dime. You ought to be able to find something as big as a missing banker."

Desmond sighed. Oh, dear, that was just like a human. Most of the time humans claimed to be able to do just about anything and everything. Then when something really difficult came along they had to ask help from the nearest dog. Warders did it when prisoners escaped, and police and hunters and watchmen had to rely on dogs to help them in their jobs. Well, it was quite natural for Gus to ask advice.

So Desmond shoved aside an old peach basket used for gathering leaves, and really bent his mind to the problem.

To make the thoughts come more easily he raised a hind leg and scratched behind one ear. That was one nice thing about being under the porch, there were no stupid grownups to rub smelly flea powder all over you, or give you a bath, just because you were trying to think. Gus didn't count as a grownup, and he helped scratch behind Desmond's other ear.

They might have gone on thinking all day, and until school started again in a few weeks' time, but Gus's mother came out from the kitchen and called him.

Desmond followed, of course, and Gus's mother gave them each a cookie.

"Now what have you two been doing this time?" she asked. "And who were you hiding from?"

"Nothing," said Gus. "Nobody."

"Strange," said Gus's mother, "because you don't look ill, either of you. Well, if you've been doing nothing, and are still doing nothing, you can stay and help me. I can always use a third hand. Hold this bowl for me."

So Gus reached up and steadied a bowl, while his mother tried to read from a book whose pages kept turning over, poured with one hand, and beat with the other.

"Mr. Titus has things that hold things," said Gus. "You screw them onto a table."

"He hasn't any Gus to help him hold things," said Gus's mother. "I'll call you if I need you again." And she gave them each another cookie.

It might have been the cookies that helped, as everyone knows they help thinking. Or it might have been that Gus and Desmond were afraid of being called back to the kitchen to help again and having to spend the morning there. Anyway, they were scarcely out of the door when they knew what they must do next.

They would go straight to Mr. Titus's house and take up the trail from there. Desmond could see that plainly.

Gus understood at once. "We'll go straight to Mr. Titus's house," said Gus. "Why didn't you think of that before, you lazy pup, you?"

Desmond grinned and trotted ahead. He hadn't been a pup for years; that was just a term of endearment, because Gus was pleased. Keeping a watch for the Sinister Stranger, he slipped through the lilac hedge. Nobody was about, and there was no car in the yard except the one that belonged to Mr. Titus, and somehow it was beginning to look a little forlorn, like a dog waiting for his master.

To show Gus that he was really trying, Desmond snuffled twice and lay his nose to the ground. He circled the garage, with Gus at his heels. In the driveway there was a strong smell of fresh car oil, left over from yesterday, and several cigarette ends.

But there was no scent of Mr. Titus. Dozens of people must have been over this ground lately, but nobody whose scent Desmond could recognize. He told Gus that, as plain as plain.

"We've got to find something," said Gus.

To encourage him Desmond stopped being a bloodhound, straightened his tail, lifted a forepaw, and became a pointer. That was easy, because he was a little bit of both. He showed Gus something that somebody had thrown into a bush—a few flashbulbs left by a photographer.

"Gosh!" said Gus. He picked up the bulbs in his

handkerchief, which was the right way, if you didn't want to ruin the fingerprints. He shoved them into the pockets of his shorts. "We'll call them Exhibit A. Now we're really detecting!"

Then they trotted round in a wider circle that included the whole house and yard. Desmond sniffed so hard that he sniffed a grass seed up his nose and sneezed. But there was still no sign or scent of Mr. Titus.

Then a car drove in. It wasn't a police car, but all the same they slipped back into their own yard, because it might belong to the Sinister Stranger.

Down in their thinking place under the porch, Gus started to do his share of the brain work—which was only fair.

"Our next step is to remember just everything we know about Mr. Titus. Then we put our clues together. They always do that," said Gus.

Desmond gave a wag of his tail to show that he agreed.

"One." Gus turned down a finger to help Desmond count, as Desmond wasn't very good at it. "Mr. Titus took his overalls. Nobody else would have taken them, they were so old and greasy." He turned down another finger. "Two. Mr. Titus took those tools off the wall. They weren't the big expensive ones that would be stolen first. Three. Mr. Titus finished that job he was doing, and cleaned up the lathe afterwards."

Desmond gave another wag of his tail. Good for Gus!

But that still didn't make four clues so you could put two and two together. All good detectives did that.

Now Gus was frowning so hard you could tell he was doing some really hard thinking. "You don't suppose," he asked, "those overalls and tools were some sort of a disguise? I mean, nobody would expect to find a banker walking around town in greasy overalls and carrying a lot of tools. Mr. Titus never did that before."

Desmond tried to help. He cocked one ear to say, "I'm listening carefully. Tell me more."

But Gus hadn't any more to tell, just yet. He got up from the flowerpot seat and said, "Now we've got to do some leg work, as they call it. We've got to explore every avenue and leave no stone unturned. Come on, you lazy old dog!"

So they set off down Rosewood Avenue and turned into Main Street. There weren't any stones to turn, as the road was blacktop and the sidewalks concrete. Desmond was glad of that, because even burying a bone was sometimes hard on the paws and nose.

The hundreds of trails along here were all mixed up. There were traces of rubber-soled shoes which smelled quite different from ordinary sneakers, and one or two traces of sole leather. He pointed out a piece of newspaper, a matchstick, and then another matchstick. But Gus wasn't interested in them. On one side of the sidewalk was the road, which gave off odors of pitch and rubber and oil and burned gasoline. On the other side you could smell flowers and, at one spot, a boxwood hedge that smelled like cats.

People said, "Hi, Gus! Hi, Desmond!" The older ones said, "Good morning!" Gus answered them and Desmond wagged his tail. There were even a few dogs, but Desmond had no time to stop and talk.

"How about trying the bank?" asked Gus.

So they turned in there. Desmond always hated revolving doors. If Gus didn't remember to keep on turning, the door trapped Desmond inside, and if Desmond wasn't careful to keep his tail tucked in, the door bit it. But this time Desmond got through safely.

There was the same old mahogany partition, with cages in which the bank kept the men and women who counted the money, so they wouldn't run away with it. There were about a dozen customers. But of course Mr. Titus wouldn't be on this side of the long counter.

Gus dropped his voice to a whisper. "He used to live in that room behind there, Desmond. You-know-who."

The door was shut, though, and it was beyond the counter. So Desmond couldn't do anything about it. On this side were two men in overalls—much cleaner ones than Mr. Titus's. And anyway, Gus knew them both. One was called Red and the other Shorty; they worked at the filling station.

Then something happened. A woman was taking some papers out her handbag and dropped her keys, which were tied to a handkerchief. Nobody had seen her drop them, not even Desmond, but he found them because his nose was nearer the floor than other people's. Because he had retriever blood, he picked them up without thinking. Because of the perfume on the handkerchief it was hard to smell which person the keys belonged to. But he traced her just as she went out through the revolving door. Then he had to stop, feeling foolish because the door stopped turning. He had to wait until somebody else pushed it.

But there, not half a block down the road, the woman was standing beside her parked car and fumbling in her bag for her keys.

Desmond put the keys right into her hand. And was she surprised and pleased! She made a great fuss over Desmond and left a strong smell of perfume on his ears where she patted him. It was going to be difficult to do any good tracking with that perfume hiding all other scents. Humans didn't seem to understand things like that.

When Gus came up she thanked him too, because he belonged to Desmond. She wanted to drive the two of them back home, but Gus said he had important business to attend to.

As soon as she had gone Desmond had an idea. Filling stations were where people went when they wore overalls. Red and Shorty had shown that. So perhaps Mr. Titus was at a filling station. That would be hard to explain to Gus. Instead, Desmond put his nose to the ground and led him there.

Gus understood right away, and asked Shorty, who had just got back, "Seen anything of Mr. Titus here, Shorty?"

"Not since he left the bank, Gus. Afore that he used to park here regular, during banking hours."

Now that Gus had the idea, Desmond didn't have to lead any longer. Gus and he went round to every filling station, the two garages, and even the body-welding shop.

But there was no news. Nobody had seen Mr. Titus.

Desmond really took pains over this leg-work part of being a detective. He must have sniffed a good hundred people, and not even one of them became suspicious that he was suspicious. Sometimes he went down-wind a long way; sometimes he began talking with another dog and just seemed to happen to pass close to the suspect. One of the most important parts of being a skilled plain-clothes dog was not to put people on their guard.

It was all quite new, and different from guarding a house. At home you could shut your eyes and divide visitors into friends and strangers just by their smell and their walk. Then you went right up to the strangers and sniffed them. Sometimes that made them nervous, because they had guilty consciences or bad intentions. Then you barked, if you knew that someone was at home; but if you were guarding an empty house you growled. You growled again if they tried to leave the path, and you saw them right off through the gate and gave them a parting bark to send them on their way.

They were back on Main Street again when Desmond heard steps behind and thought he recognized them— even though the man was walking now, and last night he had been running most of the time. Desmond dropped back and, so that he wouldn't arouse the man's suspicions, stopped for a friendly word or two with Alf the airedale. Yes, it was the same man, the Sinister Stranger. He had disguised himself by not wearing his raincoat, but Desmond could still catch a faint scent of it. He took a full list of the man's smells, from hair oil to something like the stuff Gus's father put on his chin after shaving, and of course the man's own smell.

A man's odor tells just as much about him as his expression does—whether he's tired or angry or pleased or hungry, and lots of other things. It doesn't change as quickly as an expression does, so it's more reliable. But humans haven't thought up any words for the really interesting smells, so there was no way of telling Gus. The only way was to show him.

Desmond caught up with Gus before he had time to whistle, which was just as well, because the Sinister Stranger would have recognized that *Whee-a-whee*. Desmond ran a little ahead and put his nose to the sidewalk. Of course there was no trail there—or rather, there were hundreds of trails. But Gus caught the idea right away, and followed as Desmond turned off Main into Butternut Street. They stopped and looked into a store window. Other people passed them, but not the Sinister Stranger. They hurried, they almost ran; yet when they had turned two corners there was the Sinister Stranger keeping only twenty yards behind them.

Now Gus had spotted him, too, and turned the corner quickly into Main again. "We'll have to try a ruse," he said. Whatever that was.

So they dived into a five-and-dime. Sure enough, the

man followed them in. He made a mistake, though. Instead of staying by the door he followed them right in among the counters. All Gus had to do was bend over and be out of sight. The man couldn't see Desmond, anyway, and because Desmond was nearer the ground he could see the man's feet under the counters.

That made it easy. They dodged the man round most of the store, then, while he was at the hardware counter at the other end, simply slipped out the door and raced up the street.

The best place for a boy and dog to hide is among other boys and dogs, and Gus knew just the place for that. Some of Gus's friends and their dogs had called themselves a Kennel Club, and there, in the backyard of the Ransom place, the club was in full session.

Some dogs were being groomed by their boys and some were being asked to jump through hoops and silly things like that. Never in all his life had Desmond seen so many bored dogs all in one yard. He did hope Gus wouldn't join the club and want him to join too.

Gus stopped so suddenly that Desmond bumped against him.

"Know what, you old dog, you?"

Desmond didn't. At least, he hoped he didn't.

"There's been so much to think about that I plumb forgot that Monday's the start of the County Fair. And we haven't even begun to get you ready for the dog show. You've really got to win it this year."

Chapter 4

There were dogs who had been so well trained by their mothers when they were pups that they weren't any fun to be with. Popsie the poodle, for instance, spent all her time trying to be a lady. But Desmond had never thought that Gus was too well trained. The dog-show idea was a dreadful disappointment, and he hoped it wouldn't last.

But that was the trouble. Gus had been trained not to talk when he was chewing, not to listen to the radio in his bedroom when he was doing his lessons, not to whittle a stick with a sharp knife when he was running, and a heap of other things that he mustn't do *at the same time*. That seemed to be the reason why remembering the dog show had put Mr. Titus and detecting clean out of his mind.

Life nowadays became nothing but being readied for

the County Fair. While Desmond was being groomed
he had to listen to a lot of talk about why he hadn't
been given a ribbon last year, and all the sissie things he
must do to earn it this year.

"You mustn't sit down and scratch, not ever," Gus
said, with another stroke of the brush. "And you mustn't
grin at the judge. And you mustn't get into fights, no
matter what other dogs call you. And you mustn't loll
out your tongue and look half-witted."

Desmond hauled in his long red tongue, though stick-
ing your tongue out when you were being brushed was
like grinning when you scratched yourself—half the
fun.

Because Gus had seen pictures of a famous greyhound, he wanted Desmond to stand with his hind legs
so far back that he nearly fell on his nose. Next he
wanted Desmond to make his front legs look bowed,
like cowboys on the TV. That was because a bulldog,
Champion Bertram the Fourth, had bowed legs, and had
won even more prizes than the greyhound. It certainly
was going to be difficult.

What gave Gus more trouble than anything else
was Desmond's beautiful white shirt front. Desmond
couldn't get a grass burr in it, or a spot of any sort,
without Gus dragging out the hose again, and Desmond's own bath towel, and giving him a fresh washing
and a fresh combing. When Gus heard that another

boy was using laundry blueing to make his dog look whiter, he put blueing in the upstairs bathtub and held Desmond in it for a full five minutes. He must have put too much color in the water, or it wasn't the right kind, because half of the tub and all of Desmond's shirt front turned blue.

The soap with the perfume in it had been bad enough. It was so strong that Desmond couldn't smell anything else for hours after, which was as bad for a dog as being blindfolded. But this blue stain was too much even for Desmond.

Just as soon as he could he slipped away, found some lovely black oil that had dripped from a car, and had a long, delicious roll in it. There wasn't a trace of perfume left on his coat, and nobody would even suspect he had ever had a white front. He came home grinning all over.

Then he wished that he hadn't done it, because Gus was almost ready to burst into tears.

"If you weren't my own old dog I'd kill you!" he snuffled. "Honest, I would!"

So Desmond felt very bad about it, and let himself be cleaned with turpentine, which stung a little when some got in his eyes. Of course that was followed by another bath. And there were the perfume and the blue shirt front back again.

There are times when human society isn't enough for

a dog, and this was one of those times. Desmond went off after supper for a talk with Bill the boxer. If there ever was a he-dog it was Bill. Bill wasn't likely to stand for curryings and combings and brushings, not old Bill.

But this time Bill didn't seem quite his old self. He stood so stiffly and held his nose so high that he looked as though he would trip over his own paws if he moved. And his coat was as glossy as a dining-room table. Good gracious, what had they been doing to him?

"Good gracious," growled Bill, backing off and not so much as giving a fellow a real tail wag, "What have they been doing to you, Desmond?"

Desmond looked down at his blue shirt front, which shone like a patch of summer sky, and back at the rest of him, which was glossy as the mayor's black limousine.

"Not—" each of them asked the other at the same time, "not the *dog show?*" Then they both started to laugh.

It was enough to make a dog laugh. Each time they looked at each other it started them off all over again. It would have been wonderful to roll over and over and just let loose, but Desmond remembered the turpentine wash and Gus's horror last time he had rolled.

Bill the boxer had won the blue ribbon in his class for three years running, which made him an expert on dog shows and well worth listening to. He explained how important it was to one's boy to win a ribbon.

Desmond could see that, so he asked, "How do you set about winning?"

Bill lowered his nose a little to make it easier to talk. "There's a book that comes if your boy sends away so many dog-food wrappers. It shows pictures of all the breeds of dogs. What breed are you, Desmond?"

"Most breeds, I guess," said Desmond, hoping it wouldn't hurt Bill's feelings, because Bill was only one breed.

Bill frowned so that he looked almost like a bulldog. "That makes it difficult. If you are a boxer or a cairn terrier, you look at the picture of a boxer or a cairn terrier, and try to make faces like it and hold your tail and head like it."

Bill, who had a wonderful memory, was willing to help Desmond decide what kind of dog he wanted to look like. He was too big to be a Pekinese or a chihuahua, and too small to be a St. Bernard or a great Dane. But there were so many in-between-sized dogs that by the time Desmond had tried to look like them all, and Bill had told him whether it suited him or not, he was stiff all over, and wondered if he would be able to recognize his own face again if he saw it. And he still hadn't decided.

The only thing left to do was to trot back home before Gus got anxious about him, and try very hard to keep clean, and hope that some of the blue would fade out before tomorrow. For tomorrow was the Great Day.

After that he might be able to get Gus back on Mr. Titus's trail again.

There's nothing quite like a county fair for noise and cheerfulness and dogs and humans and smells and excitement. There's just about every kind of domestic bird and beast; there are sulky racing and popcorn and hot dogs and machinery and patchwork quilts and jellies and just about everything else you can think of—not forgetting the big tents—all packed into one huge field with the sun beating down, and people coming from miles away all in their best clothes.

You could tell right off which dogs were to be entered in the show and which weren't. Those that weren't just ran around as usual, getting lost, running into the cattle pen for a drink of water, getting chased off the race track, and having a grand time. But the dogs who were entered in the show paced solemnly behind their owners, nose in air, scarcely saying a word even when they passed their closest friends. Desmond had decided to look just like himself. That was simplest, and anyway he couldn't think of any other dog or breed of dog who was half as handsome.

Gus and Desmond went up to a tent where a man sat behind a table with a lot of papers before him; pinned up behind him were more colored ribbons than you'd see in a five-and-dime store. The man didn't carry his ears well, and was almost bald on top, so Desmond wondered how he had managed to win so many.

He said, "Hi, sonny. Anything I can do for you?"

"I want to enter Desmond in the show, sir," said Gus.

"Okay. What breed?" said the man. He shuffled his papers and took up a pen.

"All breeds, I guess, sir," said Gus.

The man looked up sharply. "You can't do that, sonny. You can only enter him in one." Then he looked at Desmond and smiled quite nicely. "Oh, I see what you mean. We call it 'no breed.'" And he wrote Gus's name and Desmond's name down on a paper. And told them to be ready at three-fifteen, at the show bench, and to see that Desmond had a collar and lead and didn't get into fights.

Desmond hesitated, but followed Gus out of the tent. There must be some mistake, being entered for "no breed" when he had more breeds in him than almost any other dog in the fair. Still, if that man was the judge, he ought to know.

Now, until three o'clock, they were free to wander. And Gus had a whole dollar in his pocket. Half of it was really Desmond's, because Gus had been given it for his admission to the fair, but because of Desmond they had been passed in free as competitor and handler.

So when Gus bought himself a triple ice-cream cone he gave Desmond more of it than usual. Later, when they came to the home-cookery exhibit, after looking over the poultry exhibit, Gus bought two doughnuts, fresh and hot and greasy and sugary, with blobs of jelly in the middle, and gave Desmond one. You could always depend on Gus to play fair.

It was then, and maybe because of the doughnuts, that they both had the same idea.

"Mr. Titus is fond of machinery," said Gus. "Well?"

They trotted hopefully over to the big machinery exhibit. There was almost every kind of farm implement, painted red and blue and yellow—tractors, plows, combines, and things that even Gus didn't know, and smaller things such as lawnmowers and chain saws. There were some men in overalls, but such nice clean overalls that you could see at once they couldn't be Mr. Titus.

Gus and Desmond hung around and hung around. But there was no Mr. Titus. So they decided to come back later, and went off to the sheep and cattle pens. The best dogs are always to be found around farm stock because of the lovely smells. Desmond passed the time of day with some old friends and a few strangers, and just casually let it be known that he was entered in the dog show. Everyone seemed quite impressed. And surprised, too.

Desmond would have told them more, but Gus had another of his ideas. "Come on, Desmond," he said. "We'll go look at the household inventions. Maybe Mr. Titus will be there. He was always inventing."

Once people stopped eating their food raw, in the sensible way dogs did when they got the chance, they seemed to spend more time cooking than eating. And by the look of this exhibition, humans had gone a step farther and were spending all their thought and time and money on the things they used to cook with. There were pots and pans and mixers and slicers and mincers and salad bowls and nut crackers and ice crackers and things for peeling and washing. And not a single thing to eat, unless you counted the raw potato in the peeling machine.

A man who looked like a farmer in his Sunday clothes was turning the handle of the peeler. But he didn't smell right for a farmer, and his face wasn't tanned enough.

"You'd think it had a mind behind it," he told Gus, "the way that spinning knife follows round every bump and hollow in the potato."

"Sure is slick," Gus agreed. "Wonder who thought it up?"

"Some guy fifty or a hundred years ago, from what they've just been telling me." He gave a laugh that didn't sound very happy. "And here I've spent the last month inventing the same gadget all over again. You don't believe me? I've got mine out there in the truck. I'll show you."

Being polite, Gus followed him. And of course Desmond followed Gus.

Out in the parking lot the man opened the back doors in a panel truck and he and Gus began to look at the peeling gadget.

But there was something far more exciting than that gadget in the truck—a smell of Mr. Titus!

Desmond put his forepaws and head into the back of the truck, and took a deep, long sniff. It was stronger now, that scent, and told that Mr. Titus had either worked on the gadget or helped the man load it into the truck.

Desmond gave a short, sharp bark to tell Gus. But Gus was being allowed to put an apple in the gadget and turn the handle, so he didn't take any notice.

There wasn't any trail to lead Gus along to make him understand, because the trail stopped right here. Gus and the man went round to the driver's seat, because the man wanted to explain something by drawing it on a sheet of paper.

Desmond leaped into the back of the truck, sure that Gus would miss him and look for him there. But it didn't work out that way.

"Well, I've had my lesson," said the man, "and I guess I'll be going." And all of a sudden he was round at the back and had slammed the doors, with Desmond still inside.

Desmond barked, but the engine snarled louder. And the truck was moving.

The dog show was to open in half an hour!

Chapter 5

Desmond hoped that the man lived nearby. When the truck stopped he would leap out as soon as the doors were open and hurry back to the fair. But the truck went on and on, and Desmond began to worry. He had been sure of becoming Champion No Breed, and Gus had set his heart on it and worked hard to get him looking beautiful.

But that chance was gone now. And what would Gus do? Would he have guessed instantly where Desmond had gone, and taken the number of the truck? And suppose he hadn't? Suppose the man drove on home and didn't bother to open the panel doors and take out his disappointing gadget? How long could a dog manage without food or water? Desmond began to feel hungry and thirsty at the very thought.

The back of the truck, still smelling faintly of Mr. Titus, was dark and like a box. There were no handles on the door on the inside because nobody was expected to ride inside. Desmond tried lying down, but that jolted too much. He tried standing up and found himself skittering across the floor whenever the truck took a sharp turn.

The uncomfortable and worrying ride ended at last. Outside, there were men's voices, and one, though muffled, might be Mr. Titus's.

"Forget it, Si. And let's get to work on our next invention. Nobody'll be able to beat *that* one by a hundred years or so; lawnmowers weren't invented as early as that."

If this really was Mr. Titus, here was a friend in need!

But suppose he was wrong about Mr. Titus, and suppose the truck had been used to kidnap the missing banker! And suppose Desmond had carelessly let himself fall into the hands of the same kidnapers. Who would be left then to carry on the detective work? Gus couldn't do it alone, nor could the trooper. Neither of them had noses they could put to the trail.

Minutes passed. Desmond was beginning to wonder whether he ought to bark and attract attention, or whether that was too dangerous, when someone put his hand on the door. Desmond in the black dark turned to face that way and crouched, ready to spring. He heard the click of the locking handle and saw a burst of light as the doors swung wide. With a noble leap Desmond sailed out, clear over the head of the startled driver.

"Hey! Hi there!" the man shouted after him. But Desmond scarcely heard him.

He was free. Ahead of him stood a huge barn.

Desmond circled it, his nose to the ground. And suddenly he gave up all plan of escape. For there couldn't be two scents like Mr. Titus's any more than there could be another face exactly like Mr. Titus's. He raced into the barn through the big wide-open doors. Inside it looked like Mr. Titus's workshop, but much bigger. There was a man covering a machine tool with a strip of canvas. He wasn't Mr. Titus. But another machine did smell like him, and Desmond peered under its canvas cover in case the missing banker was hiding there.

But he wasn't.

An annoying thought struck him. Suppose the banker had gone away while that idiot of a man had stood there talking beside his locked truck? The man came into the barn now, the gadget in his arms, and Desmond stopped to listen.

"Fool dog! Must've slipped into my truck at the fair. Catch him, Hank, and look at his collar, so we can see where he belongs."

But Desmond hadn't played tag with Gus a thousand times without learning how to dodge a slow-moving human being, especially a grownup. He was out of the door and sniffing around before either of the men had even stooped to make a grab for him.

In two seconds Desmond was hot on the scent. It led straight to the first of three trailers set out in a nearby meadow. Desmond leaped in. And there, at a little table, starting to eat his supper, sat Mr. Titus.

He recognized Desmond right away, because of his
beautiful shirt front, and said, "Desmond! Why,
where's Gus?"

Desmond licked Mr. Titus's hand, he was so pleased
to see him. He sat down and wondered how on earth he
was to explain that Gus was back there at the County
Fair, and that Desmond himself ought to be getting
back right away or it would be too late to be judged
Champion No Breed.

Mr. Titus went to the door of the trailer and shouted,

"Gus!" several times. Desmond gave a low whine, trying very hard to explain.

"Lost him, eh?" Mr. Titus was a smart man, and he partly understood. "But how in tunket did *you* get here?" He put a bowl of water on the floor and gave Desmond some of his own supper.

Food can do a lot toward soothing your worries. But by now it was getting dark, so Desmond knew he must have come quite a long way in that truck, and unless Mr. Titus took him back he couldn't possibly get home tonight.

But could he make Mr. Titus understand? No. Mr. Titus wasn't used to dogs, as Gus was, and it was hard to put ideas into his mind. Perhaps he understood only machinery. He was kind and hospitable, though, and he said, "Well, we'll have to put you up for the night. It's a long way to your home, and I've reasons for not wanting to be seen in town."

Then he spread his overalls in a corner for Desmond to curl up on, and as he was washing the dishes and undressing he talked, just as Gus would have done.

It seemed that he had never wanted to be a banker, but it ran in his breed; his father had been one. He had wanted to be something quite different.

Desmond wagged his tail in sympathy. That kind of thing was always happening. Sometimes a spaniel wanted to be a fighter like a bull terrier, or an airedale wanted to be a sissy lap-dog.

"But I'd never have had my wish if Hank hadn't come into the bank, wanting a mortgage. Those last two years before I could retire seemed like an age."

It sounded as bad as waiting to get back to Gus. The night would be like a week, but there was nothing Desmond could do to hurry things, or even to hurry Mr. Titus brushing his teeth.

Mr. Titus gave Desmond a good-night pat and slipped into his bunk. "You're a problem. We'll have to see what we can do about you in the morning. I'd phone Gus's father right away, but what we're doing here is rather a secret, and I daren't bring in a stranger and his car."

In the morning Mr. Titus fed him, gave him another pat, and went off to the barn. And there amid the whirling machinery he seemed to forget all about his guest.

Desmond went up to Si, the man who had driven the truck, and putting his nose to the ground—Desmond's nose, of course—tried to lead him to the truck and suggest being taken back to the fair. From the fair he could easily find his way home. But maybe the man had never been around a dog. All he did was put down another bowl of water.

Then Desmond had an idea that was about as bright as any a dog had ever had. Gus had read about the missing banker in the newspaper. Maybe Mr. Titus could read, too, and would learn that everyone was looking for him and that he ought to go home. Then Desmond could go with him. He looked around for a newspaper. There were books in the trailer, sheets covered with drawings tacked up in the barn, and plenty of rags and cotton waste, but no newspaper, not even a torn corner of one.

Desmond ate a hearty lunch in order to keep up his spirits. Being used to Gus, who was a smart little guy, he hadn't realized how stupid humans could be—these humans, anyway. All they did was whistle and shove bits of iron into machinery, and take them out again in a slightly different shape, and whistle and put other bits into the machinery.

Maybe the lunch was what did it—sausages may be good for the brain. Desmond realized that whatever was to be done must be done by Desmond, alone and un-aided. Gus was the only human he could explain any-thing to. He must get back to Gus at once.

Nobody stopped him; they were too busy with their stupid machinery. He took the scent of the truck tires, just as Great-Aunt Matilda the bloodhound would have done, and followed the trail out onto the road where it turned left. Then the trail was lost in other tire trails, and even his bloodhound great-aunt couldn't have fol-lowed it.

He stood there while car after car hooted and just missed him. Now he needed the gift that all dogs were supposed to have, and cats too, and even silly birds: the trick of finding the way home for miles and even hundreds of miles. He had never needed the trick before and he wasn't sure he could do it.

He thought. He thought hard. He thought of a bone he had buried under the syringa bush. Was it to his right or left, in front of his nose or behind his tail? For safety's sake he left the road and stood on the grass and turned round and round. It didn't work. He could imagine that bone—it was a big old beef bone, too—in any direction.

Perhaps it would work better if he thought of something bigger—Gus's house, for instance, the house where he and Desmond had been born and had always lived. Better! Now he could feel a faint prickling at the back of his neck. He snorted to clear his nose; that might help. Now he almost had the direction—almost, but not quite.

Home had to be either up or down the road, for certainly the truck hadn't climbed those stone walls. And the truck had come from this direction. Desmond made a start, at a slow dog-trot.

Then he got to thinking about Gus, who'd be worried about losing Desmond at the fair, and maybe thinking Desmond had been run over. Now he felt more than a prickle at the back of his neck; he felt his hackles rise. And suddenly he was galloping up the road, quite sure this was the right direction.

So sure was he that when the road began to bend he

left it and took a short cut through the fields. Then he
found the road ahead of him again and leaped the fence
to follow it. A dog wanted him to stop and talk, and
snarled at him when he barked that he was too busy.
He saw a woodchuck cross the road, but for once took
no notice. Cars whizzed by. A squirrel scolded him from
a hickory tree, but he didn't so much as look up. Then
he struck a delicious smell of skunk, strong enough to
roll in. But he remembered how unhappy Gus had been
when he had rolled in the motor oil, so he kept on
galloping.

The picture of Gus hadn't grown any bigger in his

mind, which meant that home was still a long way off. Desmond slowed to a lope, which was almost as fast as a gallop and much less tiring. His nose was getting dry, and there was dust in his mouth and throat; and there was a farm and a small girl watering the flowers with a hose.

She knew right away what he wanted and turned the hose into a bucket. He plunged his nose in to drink. Delicious!

Then the next thing he knew she had tied the clothesline to his collar and was shouting, "Ma, I've found a lost doggie. His name's on his dog tag, Ma. Somebody ought to take him home."

Her mother didn't come out. She only called impatiently, "Tie him up to a tree. But be careful, he may bite. When your father comes home we'll try to trace him."

Desmond let the little girl fasten the other end of the clothesline to a tree, and lay down to rest in the shade. A short time later he got up for another drink, chewed through the line, and was off again. He heard the little girl call after him, but he didn't stop. She meant well, but he had no time to waste.

It was after dark when he had his worst moment. Cars were fewer and they had their lights on. He was in the middle of a strange village and he didn't know which way to turn. It might be because he was tired, dog-tired, or because the lights dazzled him. He tried to remember if the truck had turned here. But when he was inside the truck with the doors closed he hadn't seen or smelled a village, and the truck had turned dozens of corners on the twisting road.

He almost gave it up. Miserably he thought of Gus, in bed by now, and worrying instead of sleeping, and thinking that somehow he was to blame and that he'd never see his dog again. Desmond remembered Gus's voice and his friendly boy smell. And suddenly there *was* Gus, just a pinpoint in the distance but clear as clear, showing him the way.

This wasn't the road to the fair any longer, but he recognized it as one he knew, and in spite of his weariness gave a little yelp of delight and hurried on.

By the time he passed the school he had to slow to a walk. He passed the bank, even slower. Then the house showed up against the night sky and he broke into a run again.

It was dark. Not a light showed in any of the windows, and of course the door was shut. There was an inviting porch swing, which he wasn't supposed to lie in. But he could, just this once. He limped up the steps. Then he remembered Gus, and was just as worried about Gus as Gus would be about him. All sorts of things could happen to a boy when his dog wasn't around to look after him.

Desmond barked, and waited. He was just going to bark again, louder, when the front door opened and Gus skidded out and fell on Desmond and hugged him.

Desmond got in a few good licks at Gus's nose and chin and forehead before the lights in the house went on and Father and Mother came out.

"You old dog, you!" Gus tried to sound stern. "Running away and losing our championship!"

Father pointed to the chewed end of the clothesline. "He didn't tie that to his own collar, Gus. Desmond may be smart but he can't tie knots behind his head. He was stolen."

"Kidnaped!" Gus sounded startled. "Then I'll bet it

was the Sinister Stranger. Or the gang that kidnaped Mr. Titus!"

Mother was calmer. "Or it might be some boy whose dog was competitor in the no-breed class, who tied him up till the judging was over. I don't suppose we'll ever know, since Desmond can't talk."

Desmond grinned to himself as they went indoors. He might not be able to talk human speech, but he could tell Gus all about it first thing in the morning.

Father must have heard the click of the refrigerator door, for he called down the stairs. "Don't forget to leave us enough for breakfast, Gus," and gave his pleasant chuckle.

It *was* good to be home!

Chapter 6

But next morning Gus was so full of plans for Desmond's safety that he could think of nothing else.

"You mustn't let a stranger get near enough to pat you. You know my whistle. Don't answer anybody else's. Look behind you if you think someone's following you. And don't go outside the yard unless I'm with you."

Dog guarding boy was the proper custom. Boy guarding dog was something new. At first Desmond found it pleasant; it made him feel how important he was. Then he was afraid that Bill the boxer and the other dogs might hear of it. But worse even than this, Gus's mind was so full of taking care of Desmond that Desmond couldn't get him to understand about Mr. Titus.

Desperate means were called for. The gate was open. Desmond went to it. Gus whistled. Desmond took no notice but trotted gently through to the sidewalk.

"Hi! Where d'you think you're going?" Gus shouted.

Desmond quickened his trot, looking behind to see if Gus would follow. Gus came pelting through the gate.

Down the block was the house belonging to Chubby, and leaning against the fence was Chubby's bicycle. Desmond had a bright idea. He sniffed at the bicycle just long enough to call Gus's attention to it, then broke into a real gallop.

Gus got that idea, all right. He couldn't keep up with Desmond on foot, so he jumped on the bicycle and started pedaling after him. Desmond felt triumphant; things were going all right now. Gus could never have walked as far as Mr. Titus's camp, but he ought to be able to make it on Chubby's bike.

After yesterday's long hike the pads on Desmond's paws were sore. On the downgrade Gus came swooping along, almost on his tail, and it was all Desmond could do to keep ahead. He didn't think he could hold this pace much longer. He hadn't intended it to be a race, and there were miles and miles yet to go.

Then he had an idea. He laid his nose to the ground as though he were following a trail. Gus understood at once.

"Leading me somewhere? Want to show me something?" Gus panted.

Desmond barked, "Yes."

"The kidnapers?"

Well, they weren't really kidnapers, but there was

no spare breath to explain. Desmond barked again, "Yes."

Gus slowed down a little. Perhaps he was thinking that one boy and one dog might not be enough to overpower a gang of kidnapers—if they really had been kidnapers. But Gus had courage, and he trusted Desmond, too.

"Okay, I'll follow. Maybe we can find out who they are and report them to the police."

Then it was just hard, steady going. They passed

through the village where Desmond had been lost last night, but he knew the way now, and traffic wasn't bad because it was still early in the morning. When they came to the place where Desmond had made the short cut he wasn't so sure of the way, because they had to keep to the road on account of the bicycle. But they managed all right.

Nearing the farm Desmond was feeling very thirsty, and remembered the little girl with the hose. He tried to put it out of his mind. Then he had another brilliant

idea and led Gus right up the drive. Gus must have
thought this was where the kidnapers lived, but he rode
straight up to the door, trusting to Desmond.

The little girl came out and said, "Ma, here's the lost
doggie come back again. I'm going to give him another
drink." And the woman said, "Just so long as you don't
feed him. If you do he'll be back here every day."

She was right, of course. Desmond knew as well as the
next dog that you couldn't feed stray canines until you
had tried to find their owners. There were some greedy
mutts—he wouldn't mention names—who would go
visiting all the time if people fed them.

Desmond got his water, and as the little girl was giving
Gus a drink and explaining about yesterday, he had
time to lie under a bush and have a good refreshing pant.

Well, that was one thing settled. No longer would
Gus think he had been kidnaped, which was a relief.
Desmond had worried about all those rules Gus had
been laying down for his safety. It might even have
meant he'd be shut up indoors when Gus went back to
school next week.

Then it was the road again and dodging traffic. Gus
pedalled more slowly, and likely enough wondered how
much farther they had to go. This time there wasn't a
squirrel up a hickory tree, but Desmond recognized the
tree and felt he was getting near the end. Woodchucks
have conservative habits, and the same one scuttled
across the road at the same place as yesterday, and of

course the smell of skunk was almost as good. That meant they were almost there.

Yes, there was the barn, and in the field at the back were the trailers. Desmond turned and gave Gus a grin, meaning, "It's all right," and ran straight into the barn. And there was Mr. Titus!

He was just saying, "Hello. You back again?" when Gus rode slap in through the wide doors.

There was such a lot of talk—about Mr. Titus's being lost, and Mr. Titus saying he hadn't *been* lost, and Gus saying that even the state troopers said he was, and the newspapers. And they ought to know, surely.

Desmond went to see if there was anything left of yesterday's dinner, or the water that Mr. Titus had put down for him in the trailer. But there wasn't. So he went back to the barn, and the talk was still going on. Hank was grinning and saying, "Jim here never reads a paper." Jim seemed to be Mr. Titus.

Mr. Titus said that Gus was right, of course, and he knew he ought to come back. But he couldn't. It wasn't just because he was busy, but because he and the other men were working on something very secret. And the newspapers and the police would want to know where he had been and what he had been doing. Even if he didn't tell them they would manage to find out, and then the secret wouldn't be a secret any longer.

Desmond could see that Mr. Titus was right. A good beef bone was the hardest thing on earth to keep secret.

You couldn't afford to go back and forth to where you had hidden it; some other dog was sure to see you, and that was the last of it so far as you were concerned. Mr. Titus should stay by his bone.

But Gus had got his teeth into the notion that Mr. Titus should come back home, and honestly you'd think Gus had a bulldog grandfather himself, the way he stuck to it. Hank, the one who wasn't the truck driver, agreed with Gus. Si, the truck driver, said, "Not till she's all ready."

Desmond had not smelled a "she" anywhere here, and he could tell one a mile off. She's were people who talked about muddy paws and hairs on furniture, and often wore perfume that blotted out more interesting scents.

The trouble turned out to be that "she" had to have tapered roller bearings, or Hank wouldn't give a cent for her. And Mr. Titus wanted something else, and Si said they needed another two weeks.

"Okay, then, that's a deal." Mr. Titus pounded his hand down on a piece of machinery. "Two weeks from today, around nine in the morning, I'll go back home and demonstrate her. And that's a promise, Gus. Now how about a bite to eat before we drive you and Desmond home again? And incidentally you can tell me how, after all the resources of police and press had failed, you came to discover me."

Gus said he had to telephone home first. That was only good manners. So Mr. Titus showed him the phone in the corner of the barn, and Gus called his mother.

"I'm with Mr. Titus, and he's asked me to stay to lunch. Is that all right, Mother?"

The telephone gave an anxious squawk. Probably if Mr. Titus hadn't been reported missing it would have been all right.

Gus answered, "No, I don't know where."

That was silly. Of course Gus knew where they were. They were here, weren't they? So Desmond barked to remind him. Then the telephone said, clear as clear, "Oh, all right, if Desmond's with you."

At lunch in the trailer Mr. Titus wanted to know all about how Desmond had found him, Gus was smart enough to guess that Desmond had noticed Mr. Titus's scent in the panel truck, which explained that part and Gus told how Desmond had run all the way home and how this morning he had led Gus back here.

In return, Mr. Titus explained how he came to be here and not at his house. All the time he had been a banker he had wanted to be an inventor, and had done as much inventing as he could in his spare time. Then Hank came to him at the bank, wanting a mortgage so he could buy the barn. Naturally, Mr. Titus wanted to know what he was going to use the barn for. When he heard that Hank and Si were skilled mechanics who wanted a big workshop to work in in their spare time, Mr. Titus bought the barn for them, and went into partnership so they could all invent together. And when he retired from the bank he just moved out here, in order to be on the spot.

"What I can't understand," said Mr. Titus, "is why anybody wondered where I was. They never did before."

That was easy for a dog to understand. You could lie where people stepped over you a dozen times a day, and nobody noticed you there. But just go off woodchuck hunting, and when you got back people were whistling and calling and asking where on earth you had been, and saying that in another five minutes they'd have rung up Lost Dogs to advertise you. Come to think of it, there wasn't a Lost Bankers, was there? That might account for people getting so concerned over the missing banker.

"Mr. Titus," said Gus suddenly, "how do you start to invent?"

Mr. Titus stroked his chin. "Maybe you have a notion of something you want to make. Or better still, you think of something that people need and that no one has yet made for them. Does that help?"

Gus considered, and swallowed the last of his ham. "Whenever Mother's busy she says, 'I've only got two hands, Gus!' So what she really needs is a third hand. I'd like to invent one for her."

Mr. Titus laughed. "I'd like an extra hand, too. And maybe an extra head."

Gus explained about the mixing bowl and other things that simply wouldn't stay put. Mr. Titus listened very carefully. He slapped his knee and said, "Gus, you've got something there. I wonder why nobody's thought of it before? We'll see what we can do for you."

Gus said, "Thank you" most politely, then came back to his belief that Mr. Titus should go home, if only for a day, just to show himself, so the trooper wouldn't worry any more.

Just as firmly and politely Mr. Titus explained once more that he couldn't because of the secret. "But I'll tell you what you can do for me, Gus. You can ring up the trooper and tell him I'm all right, and will be back in two weeks, as I promised you. We can't call from here, or the police would have the call traced, and there'd be a squad car outside the barn before you knew it."

Desmond was resting as hard as he could, stretched out almost flat on the trailer floor, and thinking of that long run back. It would be hard for Gus, too.

But Mr. Titus had a better idea. "I daren't drive you myself, but as soon as you two are ready, Si can take you home in the panel truck."

So Gus and Desmond got into the back of the truck. Mr. Titus lifted in Chubby's bicycle, said good-by, and closed the door so that nobody would see them with Si. Si drove a lot more carefully and slowly than he had coming back from the fair, and the bicycle fell on Desmond only once.

Si stopped in a back street near home and grinned at them by way of good-by. Then he drove off.

Chapter 7

"First," said Gus, "we'll take Chubby's bicycle back." So they left it leaning against the fence, where they'd found it.

"But we can't just go up to a policeman and tell him Mr. Titus isn't missing any more," Gus pointed out. "He'd want to know all about it. And if he didn't recognize me he'd certainly recognize you, you old dog, you."

Desmond realized that that was true enough.

"And we musn't telephone from home," Gus went on. "Mr. Titus said that the police could trace a call from the barn, so they could trace one from our house. And anyway, Mother would want to know what it was all about."

And that was true, too.

They were right by the drugstore now. Desmond remembered how an ice-cream cone could always make Gus think well, so he led the way straight in. And Gus followed.

Who should be sitting at the counter but the Sinister Stranger, all hunched up and sucking a Coke through a straw! He had on dark glasses, probably for disguise. He didn't notice them at once, and Desmond wanted to turn right around and go out again, but that might have attracted his attention.

Gus climbed up on a stool and ordered a triple-dip ice-cream cone. So he was really going to think hard.

He had almost finished the cone and Desmond had nudged his elbow to remind him about his share of the end, when Gus whispered, "I think we'll phone from here."

That showed what an ice-cream cone could do! It was as helpful as a long scratching behind the ear. Desmond wagged his tail silently to show that he agreed.

But Gus didn't have any money left after paying for the cone. "Mr. James," he said, "will you lend me a dime? I'll pay it back tomorrow." And because Desmond had once saved the drugstore kitten—well, he and Gus had—Mr. James slapped a dime down on the marble counter.

The Sinister Stranger hadn't even looked up from his Coke!

Gus slid off his stool and went into the phone booth. Desmond squeezed in behind him. They couldn't quite shut the door because of Desmond's tail.

Gus dialed the operator, and keeping his mouth close to the phone so people at the counter wouldn't hear, asked to speak to the state trooper. The trooper answered.

Gus made his voice very deep and said, "Mr. Titus isn't lost any longer. We've found him."

"That's fine, sonny," said the trooper's voice. "Now who's 'we'?"

"Me and—" But Gus wasn't caught so easily. "Me and another fellow. Mr. Titus promises he'll be back home two weeks from today, at nine in the morning. He asked me to tell you."

"My, but that's mighty good of you." It sounded as though the trooper were trying to purr. "Now, just you tell me where you live, and where Mr. Titus is, and I'll be right around to talk to you and—who did you say your pal was?"

Desmond caught sight of a shadow outside the booth. It was the Sinister Stranger. And he had his head pressed to the crack of the door and was listening to every word. But Gus hadn't noticed, he just went on phoning. Desmond nudged his elbow. Gus took no notice.

"I didn't say who he was, because it's all part of Mr. Titus's secret. But Mr. Titus promised to be back, so he will be."

Desmond was wriggling with anxiety. Gus seemed to have forgotten what Mr. Titus had said about the police tracing a call and sending round with a squad car. And he still hadn't noticed the Sinister Stranger outside the booth.

The trooper continued to purr. "Well, thanks, sonny. And how about putting your pal on, so I can thank him, too?"

Desmond barked, though it wasn't good manners to bark indoors. He barked again, till Gus looked round and saw the stranger by the crack in the door. He understood at once.

He hung up the phone, but not before Desmond heard the trooper say, "A kid and his dog! Can you beat it!" And there wasn't any purr in his voice.

Gus said, "Ready, Desmond? We'll have to make a break for it." He opened the door a little wider.

The Sinister Stranger had his foot against it. He said, "No you don't, sonny! I've had my fill of chasing you two all round the town. I heard what you said, and you're going to tell me the rest of it, or wait here till the prowl car comes and picks you up."

With one foot against the door the man got out his pencil and notebook.

"Oh, you're a reporter!" said Gus. Desmond would never have guessed that. But it was certainly a relief. Reporters were people who came to parties to write in their papers who the guests were.

"Sure am. Now hurry, sonny, before the cops get here. I want an exclusive for the *Newtown Gazette*. Where's the missing banker? Why'd he run away? Or was he kidnaped? How'd you find him? Likely enough it was a kidnaping and the gang has made you contact man. Nobody'd be likely to suspect a kid of your age. What's your name and where d'you live?"

He would have gone on longer if Gus hadn't asked, "What's an 'exclusive'? Doesn't it mean yours and nobody else's?" Which showed what a triple-dip ice-cream cone could do for a boy who really liked ice-cream cones. Desmond would never have thought of that.

"Sure does. And that's what you're going to give me right here. An exclusive interview with the finder of the missing banker."

"I can't. Not if the police catch me first. They'll call Father. Father will call his lawyer. And there'll be dozens of other reporters at the police station."

Desmond had his head through the partly open door. It was a time for action, not for all this talk. One bite of the man's ankle and the man would jump back and Gus would be free to run. But Desmond hesitated. He had never had to bite a man before. It was awfully rude.

He didn't have to.

The man said, "Gee, son, you're right." He flung open the door. "Let's get out of here while there's still time!"

It was like old days, when they raced down the street, but this time they were all running together. They ran to the tumbledown house and dived into the cellar— just in time, too, for they saw the police car race past, with half a dozen other cars following it; one of them was marked *The Sun*.

"Now give!" said the man, and he whipped out his notebook again.

"I can't," said Gus, "because it's all a secret. But Mr. Titus will tell you all about it at his home at nine o'clock, two weeks from today."

"He's alive and well?"

"He had lunch with me today," said Gus, bragging a little.

"That narrows the search to somewhere in this town," the S.S. decided.

Desmond, who had been licking his sore toepads, looked up and grinned at Gus.

"Good, so far. But you aren't going home till you've told me more," threatened the man, becoming sinister again.

It was Desmond's turn. All he did was stand up and give one deep, sinister growl.

"Well, maybe I was wrong." The S.S. stepped hastily aside. "Guess I'll go back to the drugstore and talk to Mr. James. He'll know all about you."

Desmond and Gus strolled slowly home, grinning. Mr. James wasn't likely to tell anyone about Gus and Desmond, because of the kitten.

Chapter 8

School opened again, as schools have a way of doing. All over town dozens of dogs saw dozens of boys safely to the buses, wondering what teachers would do if there were no dogs to see that they had pupils to teach.

No dog really feels himself during those first yawning days when all the boys have vanished. Desmond got into a few fights with other dogs who called, "Blue-bib! Blue-bib! Beeyutiful blue-bib!" after him. They weren't real honest-to-goodness fights, but rather like half-hearted wrestling matches.

Of course Gus and the other boys came back home again as usual, though it was too late each day really to get anything going. And some of the boys even read books and wrote things in other books. Desmond's blue shirt front gradually faded to white. As long as Gus was really studying, Desmond wasn't allowed up in his room. All a dog could do was to yawn, and scratch occasionally, and wish he had been able to give Gus the Champion No Breed ribbon to pin up on his wall.

Blue-bib! When by all rights he should have been Blue Ribbon Desmond!

Then one day Gus announced, "It's tomorrow!"

Desmond understood at once. Tomorrow was the day the missing banker had promised to come home.

Late that evening, when Gus had finished his homework, they slipped through the lilac hedge into Mr. Titus's garden. No lights showed in the house, but the housekeeper was still housekeeping. Anyway, she had emptied the mailbox during the day. Mr. Titus's car still stood outside the garage, exactly as he had left it. It wasn't very encouraging.

Late that night Desmond gave a low growl, and Gus came tiptoeing downstairs. "It's all right," he told Desmond. "It's someone with a flashlight wrapping himself up in a blanket in the shrubbery."

Desmond agreed that that might have been what he heard.

"I think it's the Sinister Stranger. But I don't think he's sinister any longer. He's lying in wait for that exclusive thing he wants to get for the *Gazette*."

Desmond could have told the man that no exclusives were allowed to hang around the house he guarded. He'd have seen them off in no time!

As soon as it was daylight Desmond broke all rules and, trying to keep his toenails from clicking, pattered upstairs. With his forepaws on the window sill he helped Gus watch.

The S.S. did a check-up on the garage, then went off down the road.

"He won't get a coffee at the diner as early as this," said Gus.

Apparently he didn't, for he was back again very soon. Other people began to turn up. Some took a look around, said a few words to each other, and went off again. But most of them stayed. It was curious. Gus and Desmond hadn't told anyone but the S.S. and the police. Maybe the police in the prowl car had told the story as a joke on the trooper who had dreamed up a tale about a boy and a dog knowing about the missing banker and when he was coming home.

After breakfast Desmond and Gus slipped through their usual gap in the hedge and went to see for themselves what was happening. People were still drifting in by ones and twos, and those who had come first seemed to act like wild ducks in a pond, which attract other wild ducks to the same pond. People on the road caught sight of the gathering and turned in to ask what it was about, and had they found the body? One police car drove up to the house; another halted in the road. A traffic cop stopped cars full of sightseers that were trying to turn in, and made them park outside.

At a quarter to nine Mrs. Higgins, the housekeeper, turned up as usual and the S.S. got out his notebook and

pencil and began asking her questions. Then a boy on
a bicycle swung in from his paper route. The S.S.
grabbed a paper and yelled, "Missing banker returns!
Good for the *Newtown Gazette!*" In a minute the boy
hadn't a paper left for his regular customers. So he stayed
too.

Desmond and Gus were careful to keep out of the
way of the policemen. They didn't know which trooper
it was they had spoken to on the telephone, and didn't
want their voices recognized. Fortunately by now most
of the boys, and of course the dogs of the neighborhood,
having nothing to do on a Saturday, were doing it here.

"Look what's happening to Mr. Titus's lawn that he
was so proud of!" said Gus.

Desmond looked. It had been unmowed for nearly a
month and was like a hay field. But there hadn't been
enough space for all those people on the driveway, and
now they had trodden down the grass till it looked as
though a storm had bent and matted it.

"Supposing"—Gus had a dreadful thought—"Mr.
Titus doesn't turn up after all? I hope he won't think
this crowd is all my fault."

Now a laundry van drove up to the gate, just as
though Mr. Titus were still living here. The traffic cop
waved it in. It looked exactly like the panel truck Desmond and Gus had ridden in, but there was the name,
Newtown Laundry, all across its sides in large letters.
The back doors of the truck opened, a ramp slid out, and

down the ramp to the driveway drove a strange contraption that didn't look like laundry or anything to carry
laundry. It rolled on three large rubber balls instead of
wheels.

Desmond gave a sharp bark and pointed with his tail
and nose, so that Gus would know where to look. For
there, sitting spang in the middle of the contraption, was
Mr. Titus!

The crowd pressed forward and there was a little
cheer. Mr. Titus waved a plump hand and smiled, but
drove right on, and the crowd had to make way for him.
The S.S. with his notebook open and a man in a green
hat with a camera did a sort of backward dance in front
of the machine. Then the S.S. caught his heel on the edge
of the lawn and disappeared from sight for a moment,
as the machine swung round him.

The machine seemed to walk on as though of its own
accord. Mr. Titus didn't appear to be driving it. He sat
there with his arms folded and let it carry him where-
ever it wanted to go. At least, that was what it looked
like. It headed straight for a big maple tree, and was just
going to smash into the trunk when it side-stepped and
went round. Mr. Titus hadn't stirred a finger, and it
hadn't really turned, but had moved sideways and then
forward again.

That wasn't the way machines should behave. Desmond was puzzled. He didn't like them. No dog does,
and young dogs sometimes run out from the side of the

road and try to bite their tires. But a modern dog knows
that machines have come to stay, and as he is going to
have to live with them he tries to understand their
habits. Desmond wriggled his way through the crowd,
Gus following, for a closer view.

The machine was a lawnmower!

Along the track it had followed, the tangled mass of
hay had been shaved as smooth and even as it ever was
when Mr. Titus mowed it twice a week. Just to show
what it could do, the contraption now ran two straight
paths, up and down, then turned circles and drew tri-
angles and just about every pattern you could think of.
Wherever Mr. Titus faced, the machine turned. Now
he stood up, and, by golly, the machine knew it at once,
and stayed stock still for him to get down from it.

But Mr. Titus didn't get down yet. He had something to say first.

"You know who I am, or you wouldn't be visiting me
here in my garden. I said I would return today, but I
never expected so fine a reception committee to welcome
me home." Being a banker, he seemed to find speech-
making easy. "You're fortunate enough to be the first
to see an entirely new kind of lawnmower. And having
seen it you will guess my need for complete secrecy
while we developed it. Even now we have some minor
improvements to patent before we can go into produc-
tion. So please be patient with me."

The police were too busy handling the crowd to be

able to ask Mr. Titus any questions. But the S.S. had
butted his way to the front again and was scribbling
hard, and his cameraman in the green hat was busy too.
He wasn't the only photographer; there must have been
a dozen or more who had brought their still cameras and
even movie cameras along, just in case. One man even
climbed a tree behind Mr. Titus's head for a special kind
of picture.

"I had no idea my disappearance would arouse so
much interest." Mr. Titus seemed amused at the thought.
"I wouldn't be here now if my good friends Gus and
Desmond hadn't tracked me down."

A big trooper sergeant grinned down at Desmond and
Gus. "So you're the two mysterious voices we've been
looking for? I ought to have guessed, seeing you around
here before. We'll call you in for advice, next time we've
got a puzzling case on hand."

"Gus!" called Mr. Titus. "Come and take my place,
and show how easy this machine is to run."

He climbed down and whispered to Gus, and when
Gus climbed up into the contraption even more cameras
began to click and whir.

Gus sat down on the seat, and the machine started at
once and almost ran down the S.S. man, who was yelling, "Gus! Gus! We're old pals. Just a few words for
the *Gazette!*"

Gus soon got the hang of it and folded his arms, just
as Mr. Titus had. He had helped mow the lawn at home,

so he knew how it ought to be done. He swept round the outside of the flower beds without cutting a single zinnia or aster and went up and down in long beautifully straight lines, with Desmond following to point out any patches he had missed. But he didn't miss any, unless they were hidden under the heavy carpet of mowings.

Gus stood up. The machine stopped. Desmond ran

forward to say what a fine job he had done. Gus stepped down. He lifted up one of Desmond's ears to whisper, and said, "Now it's your turn!"

Desmond stared. Gus must be out of his mind!

The S.S. ran up with a thing like a box hung from his shoulder, and was talking to the thing attached to it by a sort of string. "Gus is just telling his dog Desmond how much he enjoyed his ride on the amazing new lawnmower, invented by Mr. Titus, the missing banker." He thrust the little gadget in front of Gus's face. "Tell 'em, Gus, for Pete's sake tell 'em, or the boys in the office will never believe me. It's a tape recorder, it won't bite!"

Maybe Gus didn't notice. He was still talking to Desmond, and louder now, to make sure Desmond understood.

"There aren't any levers or pedals to bother about. . . . Of course you can, you lazy old pup, you! . . . I've got to catch Mr. Titus and ask him if he's remembered about the third hand."

"Hear that, you fellows? That was Gus talking to Desmond. And there's something new starting to happen that you aren't going to believe, even if I—" The S.S. stopped talking.

But Desmond wasn't listening, anyway, for Gus had helped, or really hauled, him up onto the machine, and kept telling him. "All you've got to do is to look where you're going. Any pup could do that."

The seat was like an old-fashioned piano stool, or the stool at the ice-cream counter, and Desmond's hind legs had to rest on the flooring. But as soon as his front paws and chest were on the seat the contraption started. And Gus, who had never deserted him before, stood back and left him all on his own.

It took all the courage of Desmond's bulldog ancestor to keep him from leaping down. It took all the courage of his poodle ancestress to think as humans thought. And even then he had to call on several other ancestors to help him. It was his pointer blood that really saved him from running slap through the hedge. He turned his head to one side as Gus had told him, to look in the

direction he wanted to go. But the contraption still headed in the way *it* wanted to go. He wriggled his legs around so that his whole body would point in the right direction and his tail could stand out straight behind. And of course the stool turned too, and so did the lawn-mower. And just in time!

Where the stool turned, the machine followed! That was the trick, and simple enough, once you got the hang of it. Desmond stopped quivering with anxiety. He could hear the voices of the people running beside him and saying all sorts of silly things.

"It shouldn't happen to a dog!" "It's a boy dressed up as a dog." "No, it's too small, and anyway I know the dog—it's Desmond." "Maybe it's done by that new re-mote control." "After this I'll believe anything!"

Of course he was Desmond; Desmond who ought to be Champion No Breed. And to top it all he was Des-mond the Driver, doing what no other dog, even his own famous ancestors, had ever done before!

By keeping his tail quite stiff he mowed two beautiful straight lines. He would have gone on mowing, but the S.S. stood right in his way, and rather than turn aside and so spoil his perfect pattern, Desmond stood up and the machine stopped.

"I've been telling you fellers, and there's going to be pictures to prove it. But I don't expect you to believe me. And now I'm going to get a few words from the dawg, yes, d-o-g, dawg. He's a slick-looking black and white maybe sheep dog, and I mean maybe. Look folks, if I slip up here it's because I've never interviewed a dawg before." He thrust the microphone thing in front of Desmond's nose. "Just say a few words. I'm bushed."

Cameras were grinding and whirring and clicking. Desmond put out a long curling tongue to moisten his nose, which was his way of clearing his throat. Then he began to talk.

He spoke for a full minute—so the newspapers said afterward. He knew that nobody but Gus was smart enough to understand him, but his words would go down in history, and some day some learned men, who might be almost as smart as little Gus, would be able to interpret them. Then he turned to Gus to bark, "Where's Mr. Titus?"

But Gus wasn't there.

There wasn't any Mr. Titus, either or even the laundry van. Mr. Titus must have taken the opportunity, when all eyes were on Desmond, to slip into the van and drive off. And it looked as though Gus had gone with him. But Gus wouldn't have deserted Desmond like that, surely!

Desmond the Famous, Desmond the First Dog Driver, forgot his new importance and became just a dog who had lost his boy. He shot down off the machine and streaked through the crowd. He circled the house, he sniffed inside Mr. Titus's car. He even looked inside the empty police car: no Gus.

The side door of the garage was closed as usual, but the padlock wasn't through the hasp. And here was Gus's scent, that pleasant, friendly boy scent. Desmond jumped up and rattled the door with his forepaws and Gus opened it.

"Mr. Titus has slipped away," he told Desmond, though Desmond knew that already. "But he left this third hand, and wants Mother to try it out, so he can improve it later."

Gus took the thing out of its box and laid it on the saw bench. He leaned his stomach against a slide and, sure enough, two rubber-covered clamps came together, and looked as though they would hold something. But Desmond wasn't interested. What he needed after all this excitement was a long drink of water, and a bone he had stored under the syringa bush. There is nothing so soothing as gnawing on a good ripe bone.

Gus must have felt the same way, except for the bone. For he said, "We can't go home yet. Half of Newtown would follow us, asking questions about how old I am, and how long we've known Mr. Titus, and what grade I am in school, and what you eat."

Then suddenly he looked startled. "Oh, gee, Mr. Titus's new lawnmower! Those people will have it all to pieces if we're not quick." And he bolted through the door.

Desmond started after him, then remembered and turned back. Gus seemed fond of this stupid third hand.

There was only one thing to do. After all, his second great-uncle had been a retriever, hadn't he? He put his jaws on the wooden thing and tried to lift it. It wouldn't come. He braced his forepaws against the bench and gave a tug. Now it came. He laid it on the floor and walked around to try to find the best jawhold on it. A good retriever always pretends to be carrying an egg in his mouth. Desmond did the same. Holding it so gently that his teeth wouldn't leave a single mark on the varnish, he shot out through the door and made for home. He took it to the syringa bush, because that was where he always buried his valuables. But there was no time to bury it now.

Back again he went to Mr. Titus's garden to tell Gus.

Gus was too busy to listen. The police had shoved Mr. Titus's car out of the way and opened the big garage doors, and Gus was driving the lawnmower in; there was just room for it. The big doors rattled down. Desmond was waiting at the side door when Gus came out and fastened the padlock.

It was like old times when they raced past the back of the garage, the back of Mr. Titus's house, and the back of their own house to the syringa bush. They looked back to see if the S.S. was following them as usual. But no one was.

There was the third hand, exactly where Desmond had hidden it. He asked plain as plain if Gus wanted it buried. But he didn't. He grabbed it up and said, "Gee, you're the smartest pup in all Newtown!" and rushed into the house.

Gus's mother tried the gadget and said, "You two and Mr. Titus! Whatever will you think of next?" She was just as pleased as Gus.

That afternoon Gus and Desmond hid in the woodshed, because the telephone kept ringing and it was easier for Father to say, "No, they're not here, and I don't know where they are," than to keep on answering questions.

It had been a long day and a full day. Desmond was eating his supper out on the back porch and Gus was allowed to bring out his bowl of cereal and join him. They still hadn't finished thinking over all that had happened, and it is easier if two people help each other think.

Gus's spoon clicked against something in his bowl, and he fished it out and polished it against his shirt. Desmond poked his head up under Gus's arm to see what the thing was. He knew that there were often "prizes" in cereal boxes, though he couldn't think why. Sometimes they were crunchy objects, but their flavor was poor. This one was hard and silvery and looked like a policeman's badge, only smaller, and it smelled of milk.

Gus hooked it on to Desmond's collar. He said, "Know what you are, you old pup, you? It's written here on the badge. You're a Private Eye."

Desmond tried to look at it again, but it was under his chin. Then he grinned. Private Eye wasn't far wrong, though it ought to have said Private Nose. Still, none of the other dogs could read, so it didn't matter, and it was far better than a blue ribbon. Blue ribbons were fairly common around town since the fair.

Gus set his bowl on the floor and went in to tell mother about Desmond's badge. Desmond finished the cereal for him. He didn't want Gus to be in trouble for not eating his supper. Not on this wonderful day.